The Story of Prince George

Daddy Pig is saying
goodnight to Peppa
and George.
"Just one more dance,"
chuckles Daddy Pig.
"It's nearly bedtime."

"It **is** bedtime, Daddy Pig!"
says Mummy Pig.
"They are almost asleep,"
says Daddy Pig.

"Why don't I put Peppa
and George to bed?"
says Mummy Pig.

"Can we have a bedtime
story first?" says Peppa.

"OK," says Mummy Pig,
"but only if you promise to go
straight to sleep afterwards."

"We promise!" cries Peppa.
"Story!" giggles George.

"Once upon a time," Mummy Pig begins,
"there was a fairytale castle . . ."

The castle was home to a
brave prince called George and
a clever princess called Peppa.

Prince George and Princess Peppa spent their days exploring the castle. They even had a cook who made them jellies, cookies and fairy cakes with cherries on top.

Prince George and Princess Peppa always ate everything.

When they were finished exploring and eating, Prince George and Princess Peppa summoned the royal wizard.

Abracadabra!

The wizard wore a cloak covered in stars. He put on big magic shows and his tricks never went wrong. Ever!

Everybody loved living in the fairytale castle . . . until one day a big, **scary** dragon arrived!

Princess Peppa squealed. Her royal friends ran as fast as their legs could carry them. Only Prince George stayed to face the dragon.

Princess Peppa peered out of the castle window. The dragon was very big and scary. She hoped it wouldn't eat Prince George.

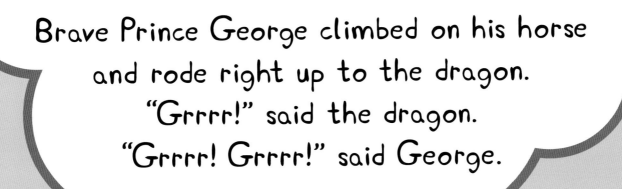

Brave Prince George climbed on his horse
and rode right up to the dragon.
"Grrrr!" said the dragon.
"Grrrr! Grrrr!" said George.

Grrr!

Suddenly Prince George giggled. The dragon wasn't scary. It was just lonely!

"Dine-saw!" cried George.

Dine-saw!

Princess Peppa came out of the castle and Prince George invited the dragon to a picnic. The royal cook made a feast. The royal wizard put on a special magic show.

Soon everybody in the kingdom wanted to meet the dragon.

Princess Peppa and Prince George held a big party and the dragon was the guest of honour. His spines popped lots of balloons, but nobody minded.

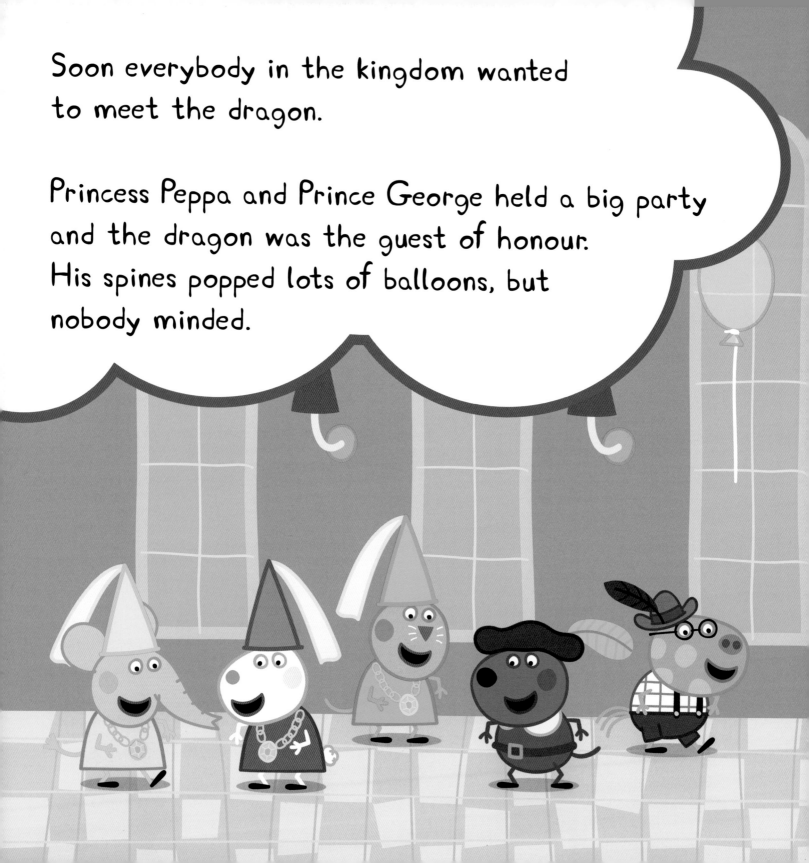

The dragon liked the prince and the princess so much, he decided to be their royal pet. Prince George led a parade to celebrate.

Everybody cheered.
Hooray for the dragon!
Hooray for Princess Peppa!
Hooray for Prince George the Brave!

Hooray!

"The end!" cries Peppa.
"Dine-saw!" snorts George.
Daddy Pig comes in to check on them.

Snore!

Snore!

Mummy Pig has spent so
long telling the story that she's fallen asleep!
Goodnight, Mummy Pig! Goodnight, Princess Peppa!

Goodnight, Prince George!